POSSUM
and the PEEPER

Words and pictures by Anne Hunter

Houghton Mifflin Company
Boston

www.hmco.com/trade

Library of Congress Cataloging-in-Publication Data
Hunter, Anne.
Possum and the peeper / written and illustrated by Anne Hunter.
p. cm.
Summary: When Possum is awakened on the first day of spring
by a loud noise that won't stop, he and all the other animals,
who have also had their winter's sleep disturbed,
set out to discover who is making all the racket.
RNF ISBN 0-395-84631-5   PAP ISBN 0-618-07030-3
[1. Opossums — Fiction. 2. Frogs — Fiction. 3. Animals — Fiction.
4. Spring — Fiction. I. Title.
PZ7.H916555Ph 1998
[E] — DC21 97-9470 CIP AC

Manufactured in the United States of America
WOZ 10 9 8 7 6 5 4 3

To Forrest

Peep! Peep! Peep!

Possum opened one small eye. What was that noise?

He buried his head deeper in his warm winter nest.

Peep! Peep! Peep!

"I'll never get back to sleep with all that racket," he said. "I'm going to go find out who's being so inconsiderate so early in the spring."

Possum stepped out into the cool, green morning.

Peep! Peep! Peep!

Possum looked up.

A pair of catbirds were building their nest high in a tree among the new leaves.

"Is that you peeping up there?" demanded Possum.

"Not us," said the catbirds. "We can scarcely hear ourselves sing with all that clamor."

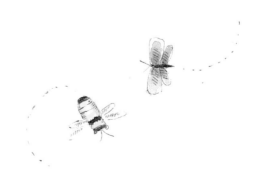

"Well, I'm going to go see for myself who's making such an awful din."

"We'll come, too," said the catbirds. "We can search high in the trees while you look low on the ground." They set off through the woods.

Possum stopped to sniff the
trout lilies blooming along the path.
Peep! Peep! Peep!
They followed the noise up a hill.

At the crest of the hill stood a
bear blinking blearily outside his cave.

"Who woke me from my warm winter
sleep?" he snarled, showing his long
white teeth.

"Was it YOU?" he said, spying Possum.

"No," said Possum, "but we are on our
way to find out who it was."

"I had better come along then," growled
the bear. "You may need someone of my
size when you find this fellow."

They continued over the hill, the catbirds flying overhead, the bear grumbling along behind.

The spring sun shone down warm on their feathers and fur.
Peep! Peep! Peep! The sound was getting louder and louder.

They came down to a marsh where they saw a muskrat spring-cleaning his house.

"Excuse us!" shouted Possum. "Have you been peeping?"

"**What?**" yelled the muskrat. "I can't hear you over all that noise!"

"Well, we're on our way to put a stop to it once and for all," said the bear, "if you could show us the way through this swamp."

They pressed on, following the muskrat, peering between new green

shoots and into dark pools. Closer and closer. Louder and louder.

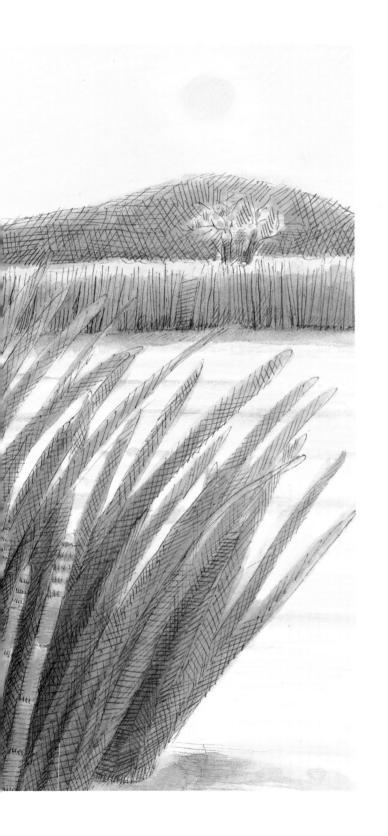

Possum pushed aside some reeds.

"**AH HA!**" they cried, squinting at a small spot on the bank.

"How could such a speck of a thing make such a huge racket?" asked the bear.

"You have woken up the entire forest, little frog," said Possum.

The little peeper looked up, from the possum to the muskrat to the catbirds and finally to the bear. Then he puffed out his tiny throat.

"**Rise and shine!**" he shouted. "**Shake a leg! Build your nests and clean your burrows! It's spring! It's spring! It's spring!**"

The bear stepped closer to the little frog. "I," he growled, "don't like to be awakened so early in the year, especially," he added, "by a frog."

"Oh, but look at the beautiful spring flowers," cried the peeper,
"and sniff the good spring smells. How could you want to sleep through
such a glorious spring day?"

The animals looked around at the budding trees. They smelled the

blooming flowers and felt the warm sun shining. They listened to the
buzzing bees and warbling birds. Legs stretched and bellies rumbled.
It was true, quite true. No one could deny that it was a fine thing
indeed to be out and about on the first warm day of spring.

"There's nothing quite like a good walk on a spring morning," proclaimed Possum. "Won't you join us for breakfast, little peeper?"

But the spring peeper was already peeping again at the top of his lungs. **"Time for breakfast! Toast and tea! The early bird gets the worm!"** **Peep! Peep! Peep!**

Peep! Peep! Peep!

DRAW
50 CREEPY
CRAWLIES

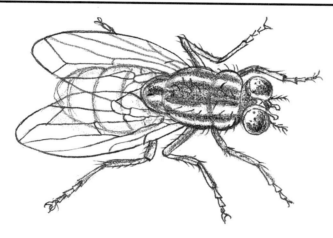

BOOKS IN THIS SERIES

Draw 50 Airplanes, Aircraft, and Spacecraft
Draw 50 Animals
Draw 50 Athletes
Draw 50 Beasties and Yugglies and Turnover Uglies and Things That Go Bump in the Night
Draw 50 Boats, Ships, Trucks, and Trains
Draw 50 Buildings and Other Structures
Draw 50 Cars, Trucks, and Motorcycles
Draw 50 Cats
Draw 50 Creepy Crawlies
Draw 50 Dinosaurs and Other Prehistoric Animals
Draw 50 Dogs
Draw 50 Endangered Animals
Draw 50 Famous Caricatures
Draw 50 Famous Cartoons
Draw 50 Famous Faces
Draw 50 Flowers, Trees, and Other Plants
Draw 50 Holiday Decorations
Draw 50 Horses
Draw 50 Monsters, Creeps, Superheroes, Demons, Dragons, Nerds, Dirts, Ghouls, Giants, Vampires, Zombies, and Other Curiosa . . .
Draw 50 People
Draw 50 People of the Bible
Draw 50 Sharks, Whales, and Other Sea Creatures
Draw 50 Vehicles

DRAW 50 CREEPY CRAWLIES

LEE J. AMES
with
RAY BURNS

MAIN
STREET
BOOKS

DOUBLEDAY

NEW YORK LONDON TORONTO SYDNEY AUCKLAND

A MAIN STREET BOOK
PUBLISHED BY DOUBLEDAY
a division of Bantam Doubleday Dell Publishing Group, Inc.
1540 Broadway, New York, New York 10036

MAIN STREET BOOKS, DOUBLEDAY, and the portrayal of a
building with a tree are trademarks of Doubleday, a division
of Bantam Doubleday Dell Publishing Group, Inc.

Library of Congress Cataloging-in-Publication Data

Ames, Lee J.
Draw 50 creepy crawlies/Lee J. Ames with Ray Burns. —1st ed.
p.   cm.
Summary: Step-by-step instructions for drawing fifty different insects, spiders, and
other crawling or flying creatures.
1. Insects in art—Juvenile literature. 2. Animals in art—Juvenile literature. 3.
Drawing—Technique—Juvenile literature. [1. Insects in art. 2. Animals in art. 3.
Drawing—Technique.] I. Burns, Raymond, 1924– . II. Title. III. Title: Draw fifty
creepy crawlies.
NC783.A44   1991
743′.6—dc20   90-19396   CIP   AC

ISBN 0-385-41189-8 (HC)
ISBN 0-385-42449-3 (PB)

SEPTEMBER 1992
FIRST PAPERBACK EDITION

20 19 18 17 16 15 14 13 12

TO THE READER

This is number twenty in our "Draw 50" series. This is the twentieth time I've had the fun and privilege of showing you a way of creating drawings. This time it's the method used by Ray Burns and myself. Working with Ray, and bringing his unique talent to the book, made this a most delightful experience.

Ray is a top illustrator of our time. In your library and bookstore, you will find many books that have been enhanced by his talent. In black and white, in full color, from cartoons to fantasy to realism, from fairy tales to history to natural science, he has shown himself to be an expert. Thank you, Ray, for joining with me in this project!

When you start working, I would recommend you use clean white bond paper or drawing paper and a pencil with moderately soft lead (HB or No. 2). Keep a kneaded eraser (available at art supply stores) handy. Choose the creepy crawly you want to draw and then, very lightly and very carefully, sketch out the first step. Also very lightly and carefully, add the second step. As you go along, study not only the lines but the spaces between the lines. Size your first steps as closely as possible to the lines and the spaces in the book—not too large, not too small. Remember, the first steps must be constructed with the greatest care. A mistake here could ruin the entire drawing.

As you work, it's a good idea to hold a mirror to your sketch from time to time. The image in the mirror frequently shows distortion you might not have noticed otherwise.

In the book, new steps are printed darker than the previous steps. This is so they can be clearly seen. But you should keep your construction steps very light. Here's where the kneaded eraser can be useful. You can use it to lighten a pencil stroke that is too dark.

When you've completed all the steps, and when you're sure you have everything the way you want it, complete the drawing with firm, strong penciling. If you like, you can go over this with India ink (applied with a fine brush or pen), or a permanent fine-tipped ballpoint or felt-tipped marker. When your work is thoroughly dry, you can then use the kneaded eraser to clean out all the underlying pencil marks.

Always remember that even if your first attempts at drawing do not turn out the way you'd like, it's important to *keep trying*. Your efforts *will* eventually pay off and you'll be pleased by what you can accomplish.

I sincerely hope you will improve your drawing skills and have a great time working on these creepers and crawlers.

LEE J. AMES

TO THE PARENT OR TEACHER

In fourth grade, many years ago, we were given an assignment to draw something to honor President Lincoln's birthday. An immediate competition developed among the four or five class artists. Which of us could draw the best portrait of Honest Abe?

We, of course, would not agree that any other one of us did the best. Our pride led each of us to consider himself the winner. Today I couldn't honestly make the judgment call that mine deserved to be number one, but I did learn something that ultimately resulted in the "Draw 50" books.

I learned the importance of peer approval. The encouragement given to us artists by the rest of the class and the praise we gave one another was heady inspiration. Most of the group went on to become successful professionals.

All the drawings of Abraham Lincoln that the class artists made were copied from other sources. This despite general disapproval of "copying." We copied from the Lincoln penny; from a five-dollar bill; from a calendar; and from sale advertisements in the newspaper. We copied someone else's work, stroke by stroke, and we erased and reworked. Many considered this to be a noncreative, harmful way to learn drawing. But we liked what we finally got. Our friends and classmates liked what we did and we were encouraged. We were on a roll, and that was of overriding importance.

Later we were able to learn technique, theory, media, and much more with the gift of incentive provided by friends, classmates, and family. Early on we copied, then we found ways to do our own original things.

Mimicry is prerequisite to creativity!

It is my hope that my readers will be able to come up with drawings that will bring them gratifying approval from friends, classmates, and family. After that I look forward to the competition.

Enjoy!

LEE J. AMES

DRAW
50 CREEPY
CRAWLIES

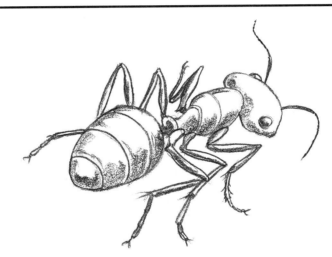

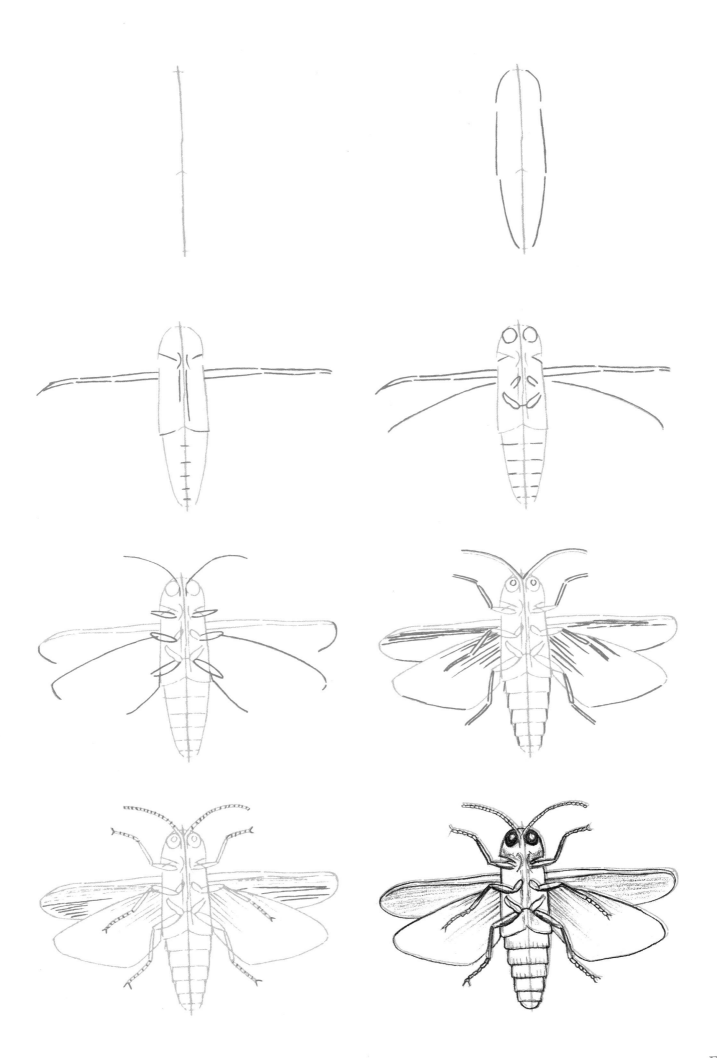

Firefly

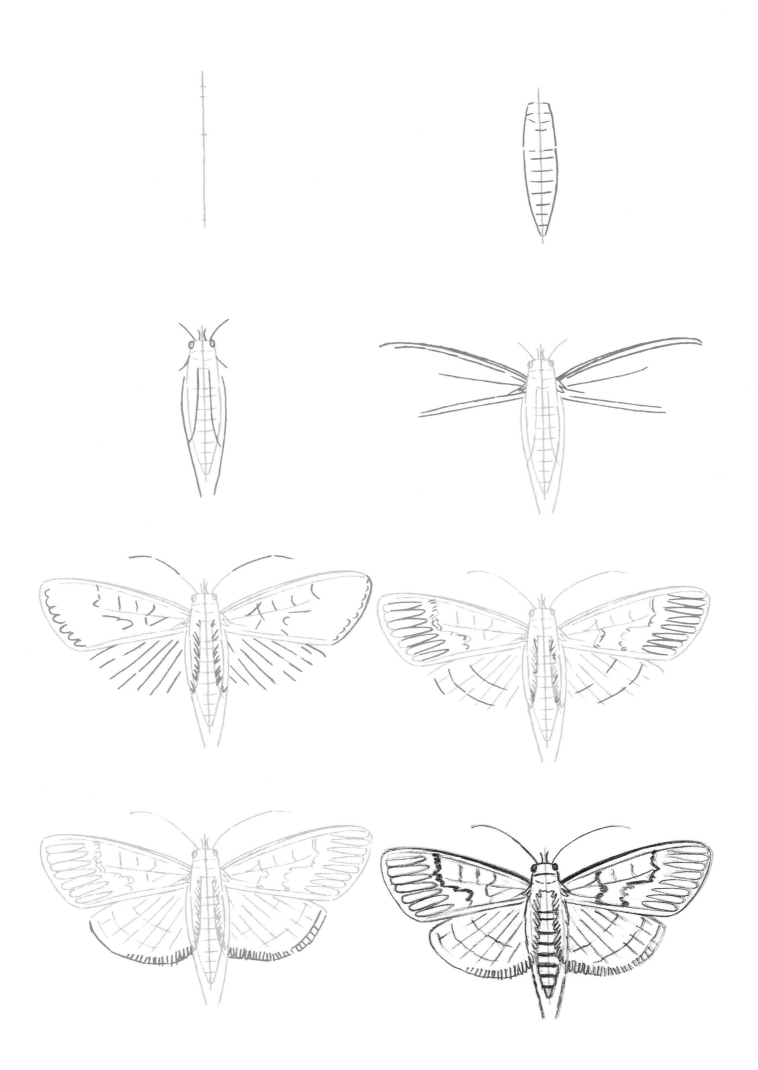

European Corn Borer Moth

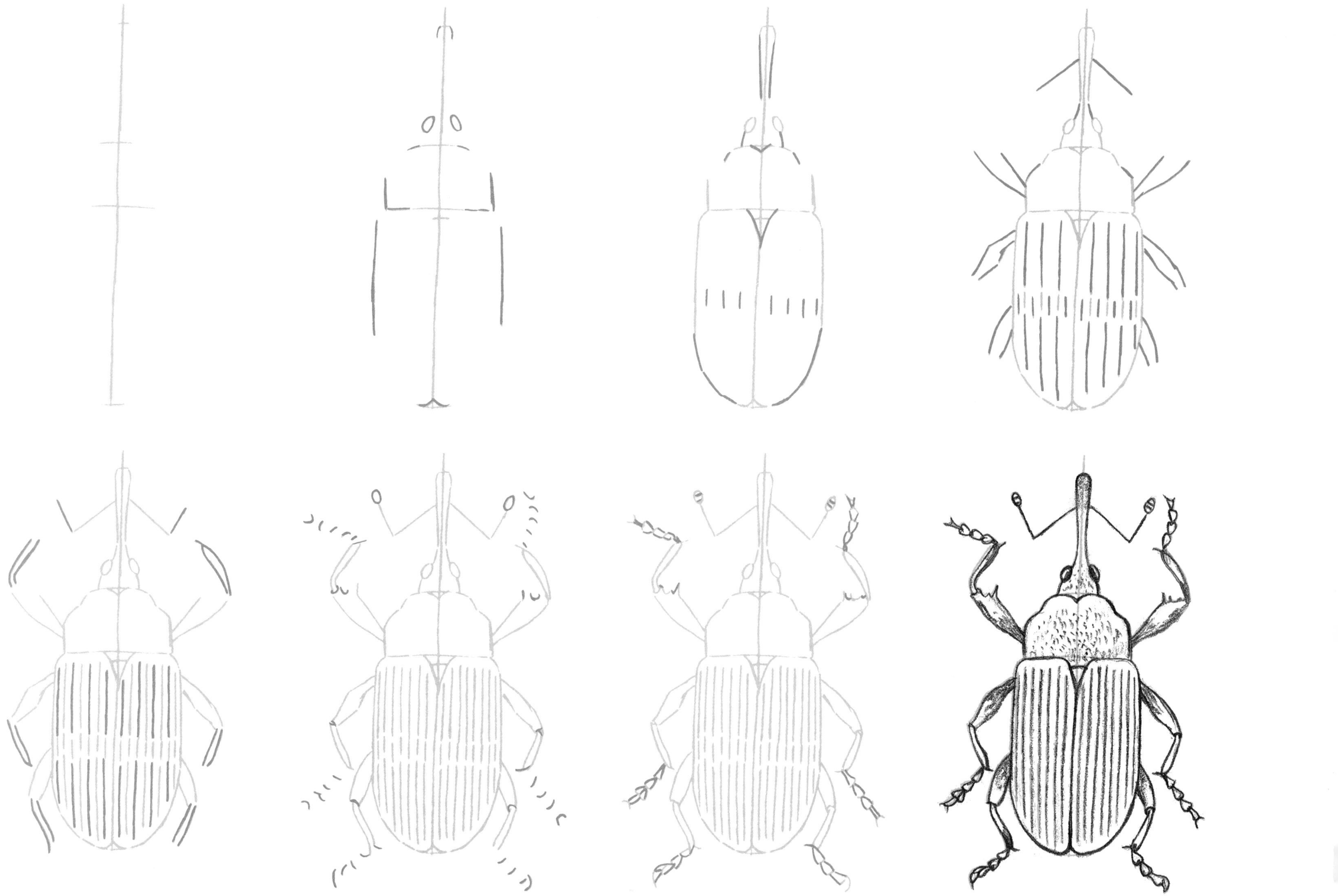

Boll Weevil

Winged Termite

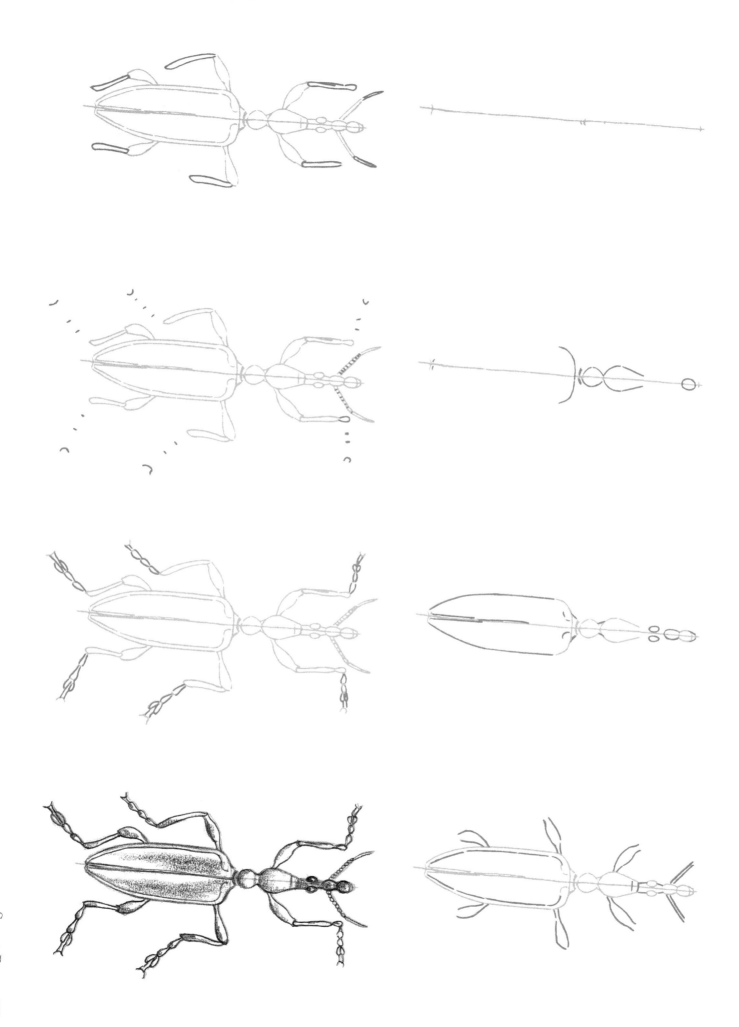

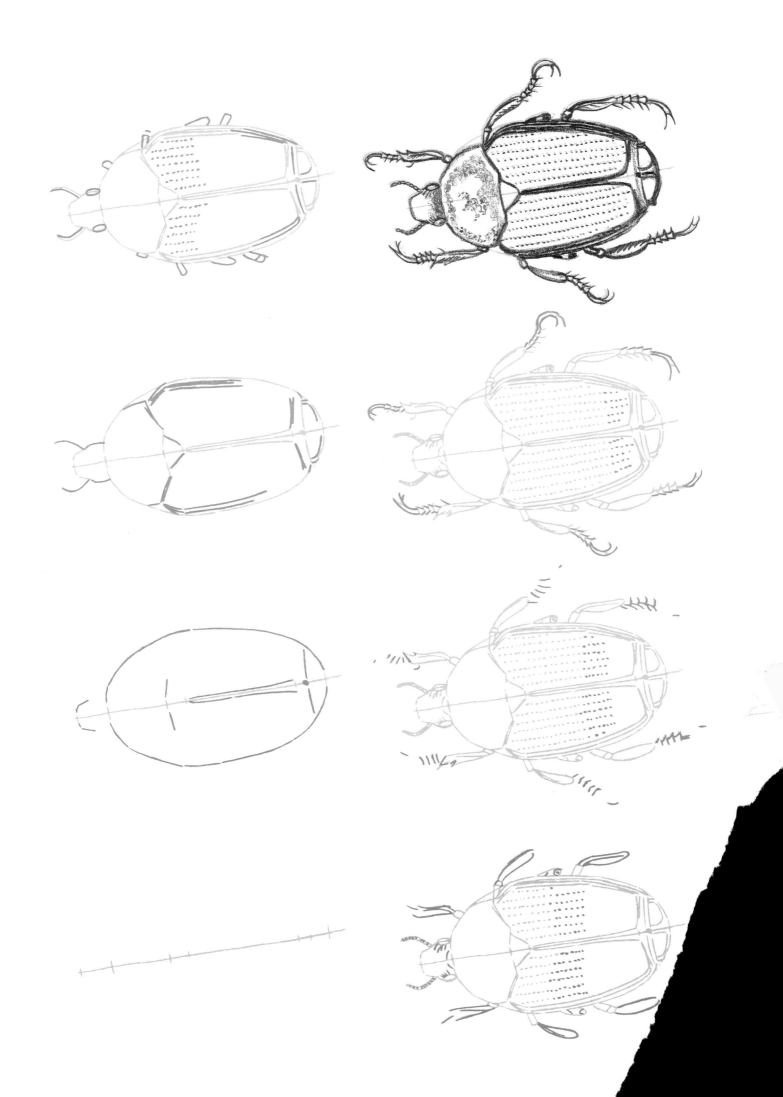

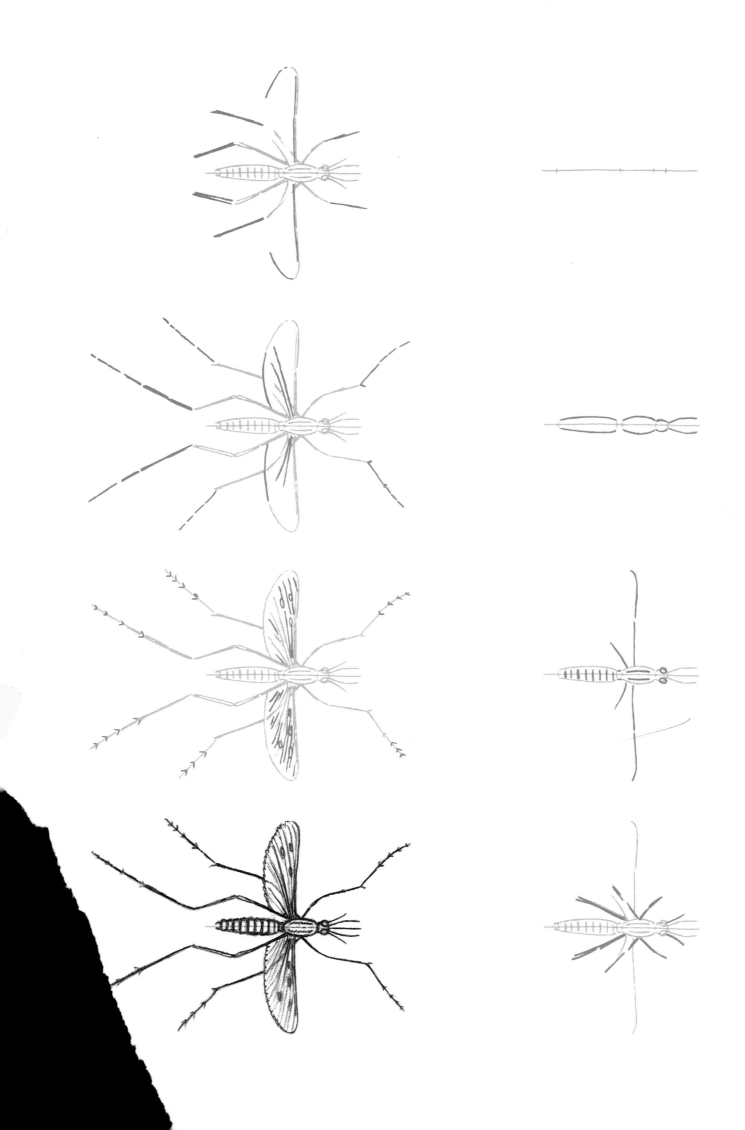

Gypsy Moth Larva

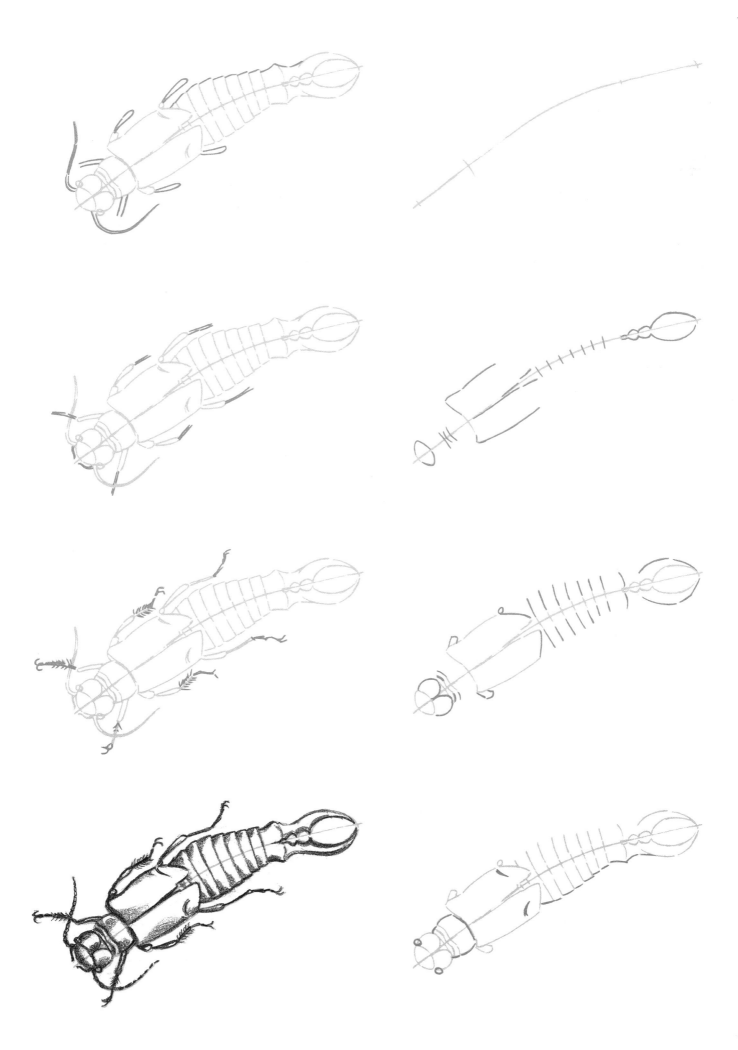

Unicorn Beetle

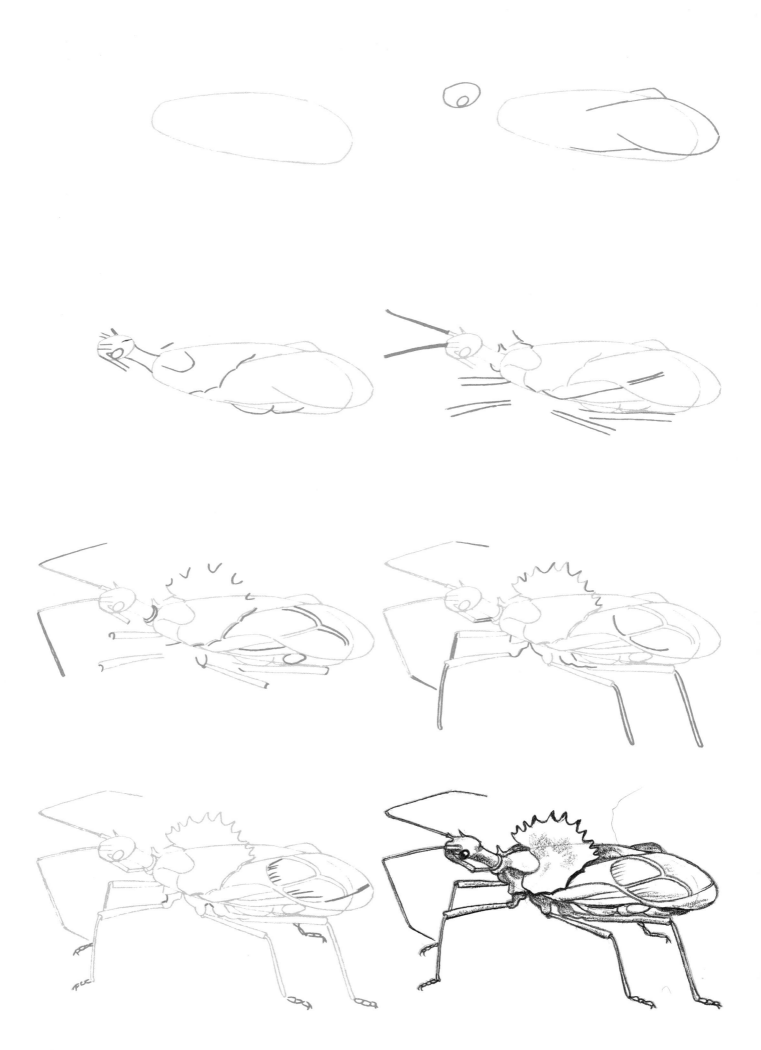

Assassin Bug

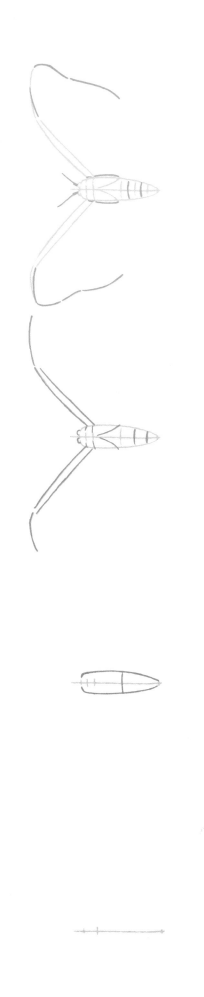

Luna Moth

Walking Stick

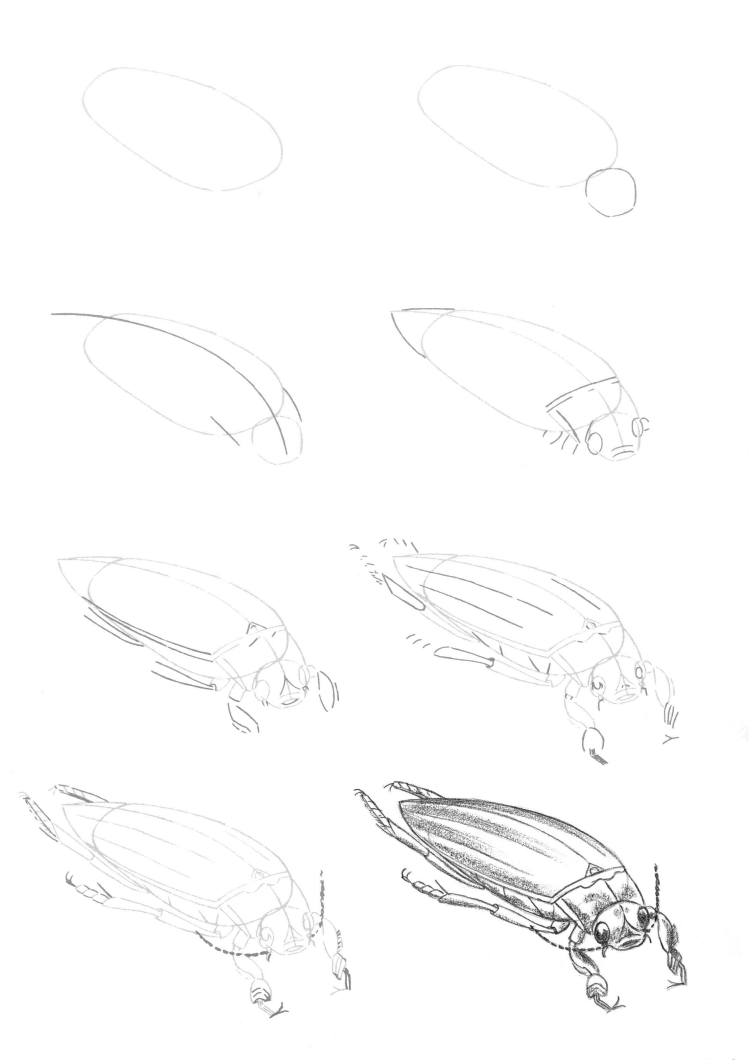

Predacious Diving Beetle

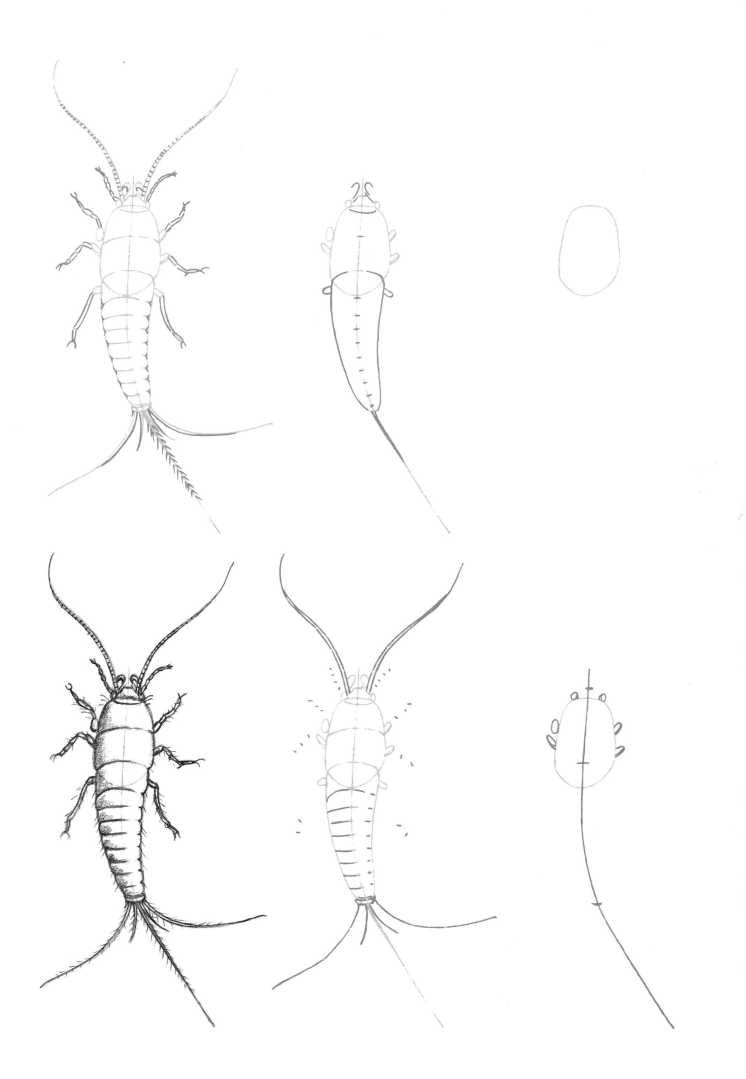

Silverfish

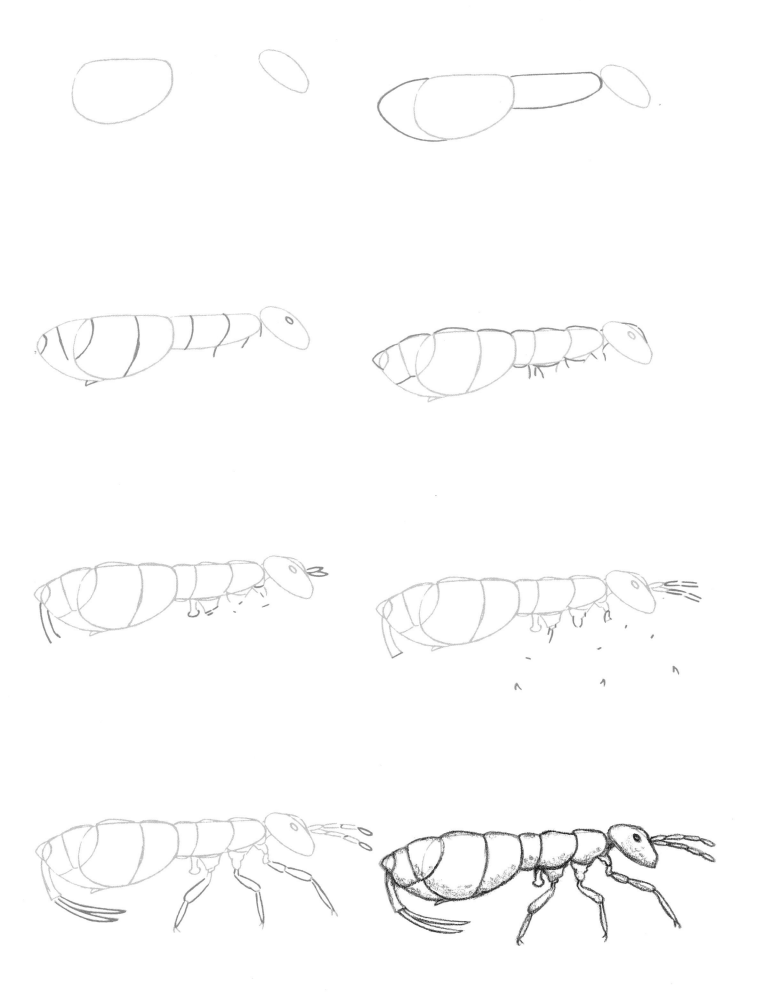

Springtail

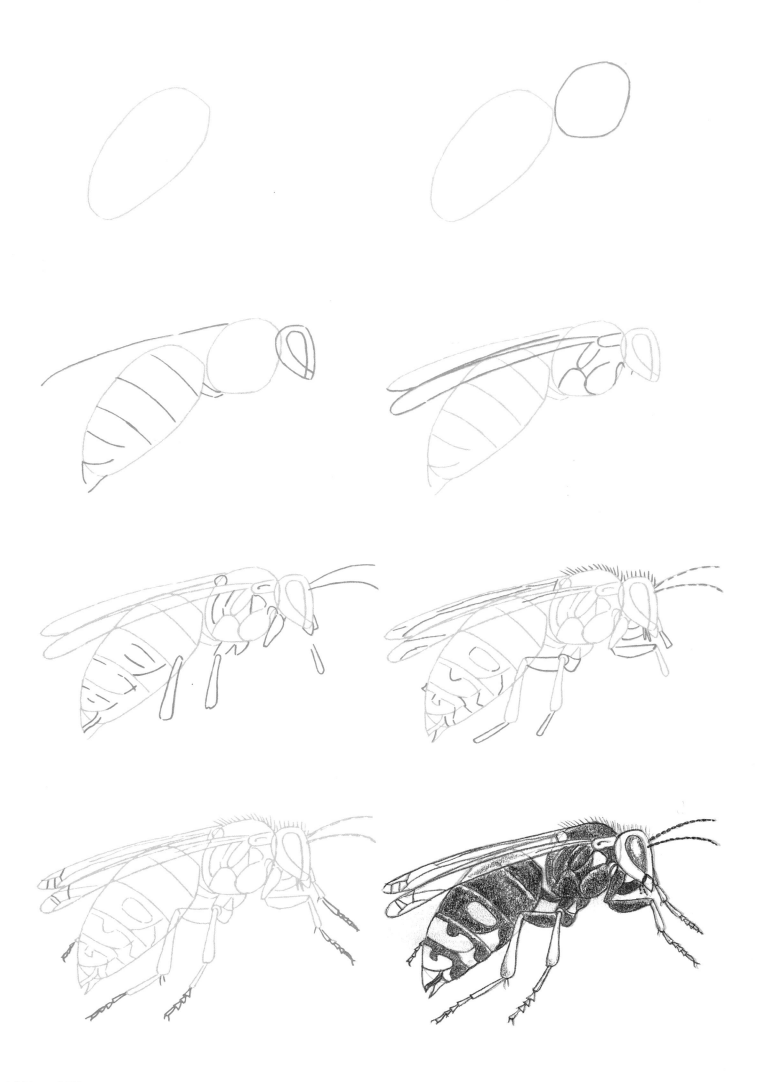

Bald-Faced Hornet

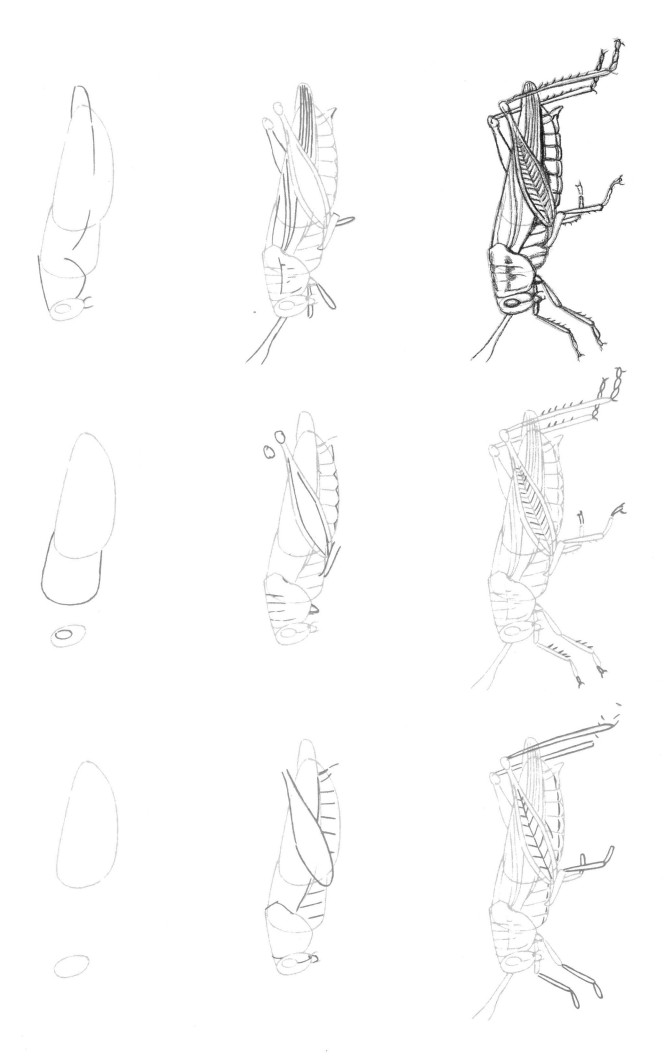

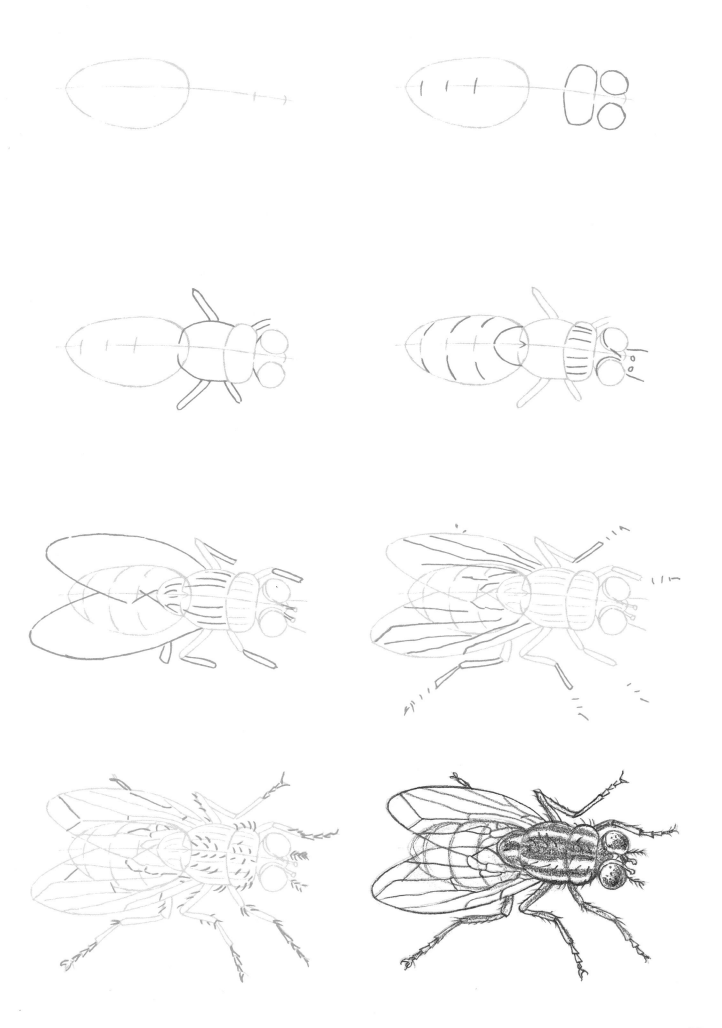

Housefly

American Cockroach

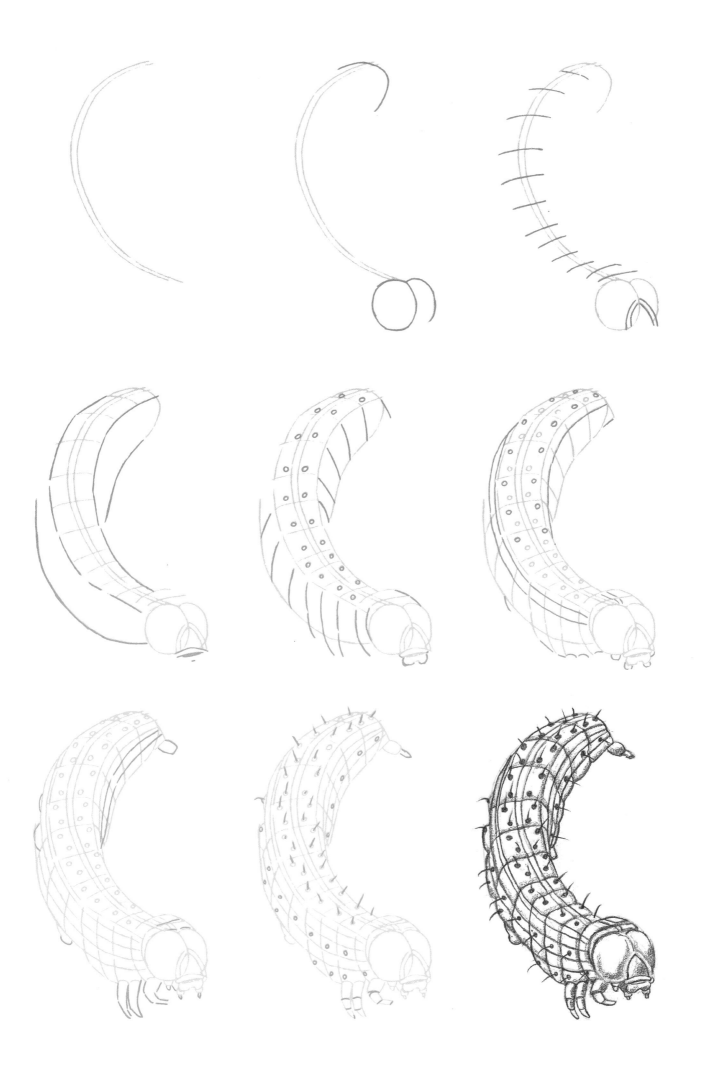

Army Worm

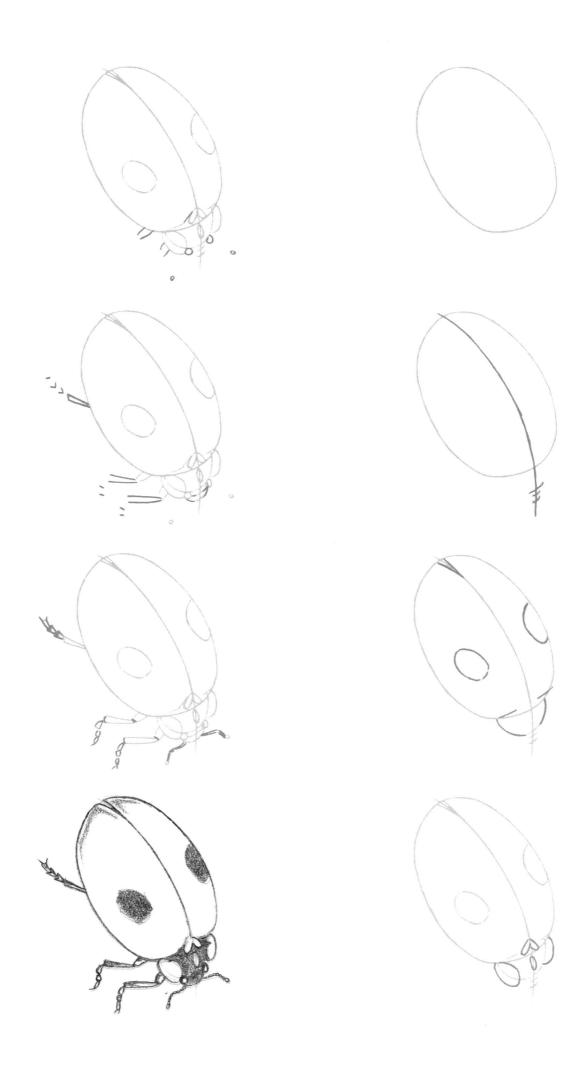

Ladybug

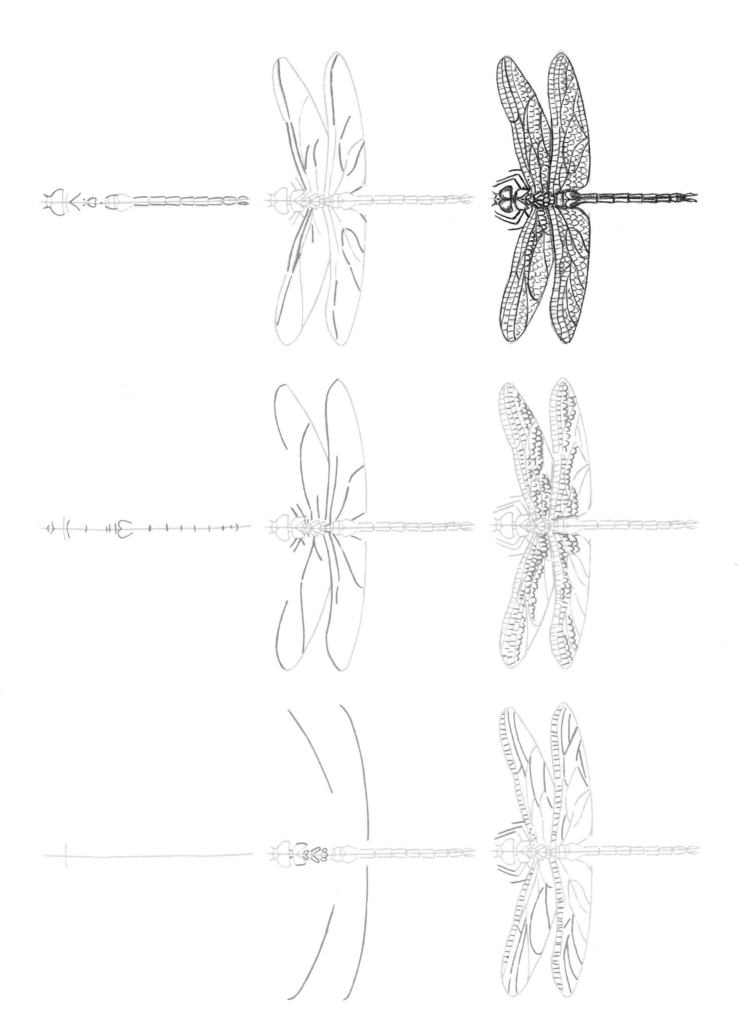

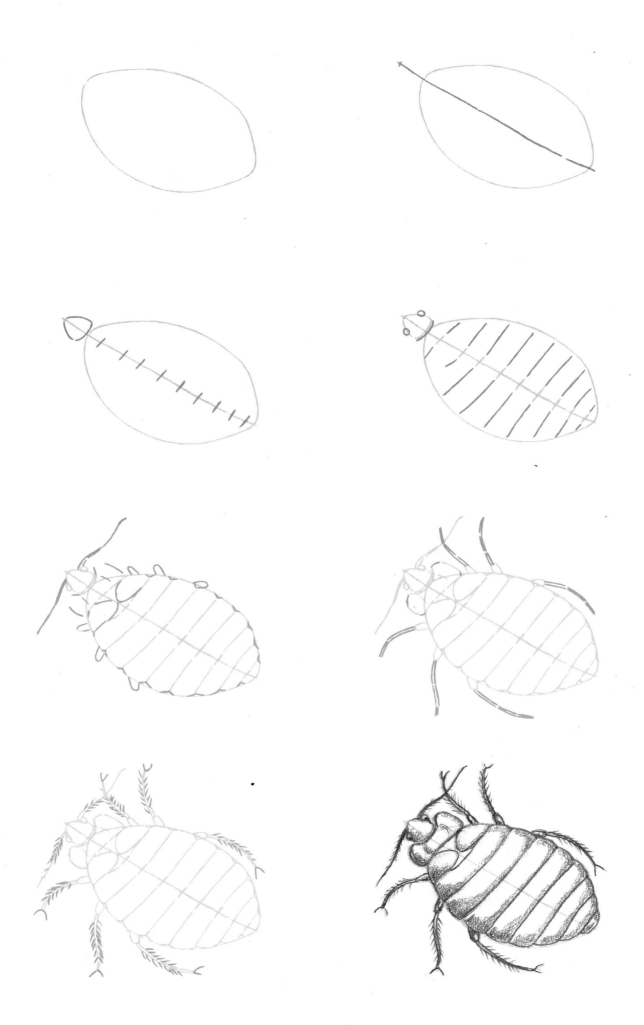

Bedbug

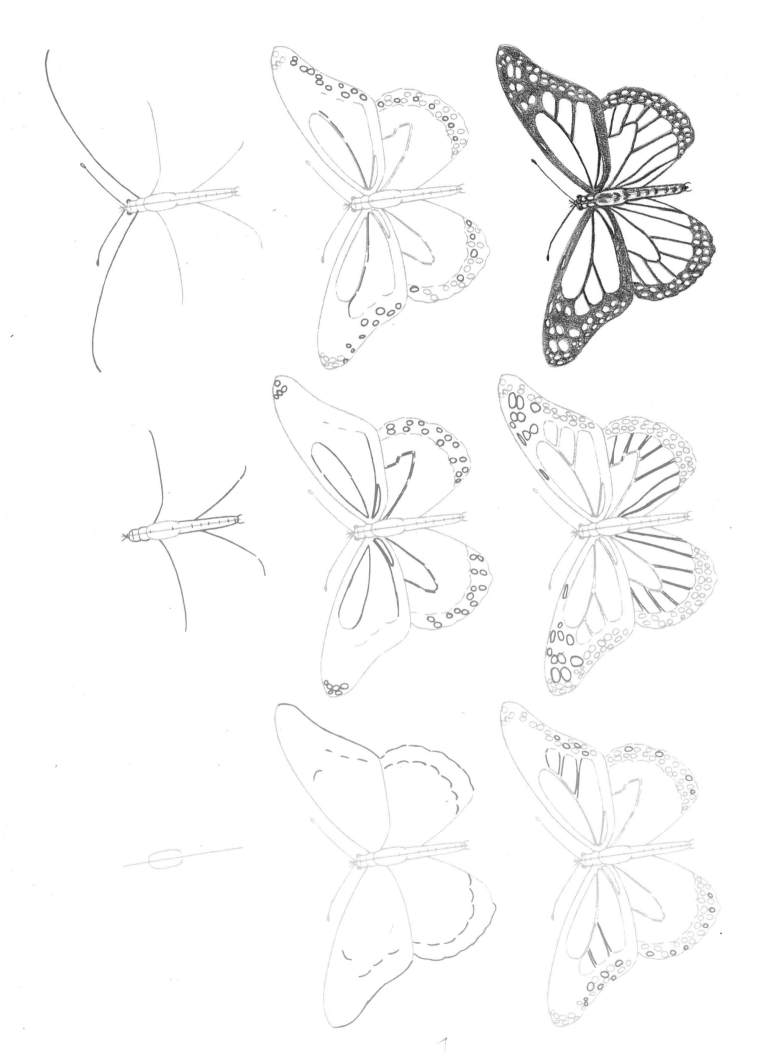

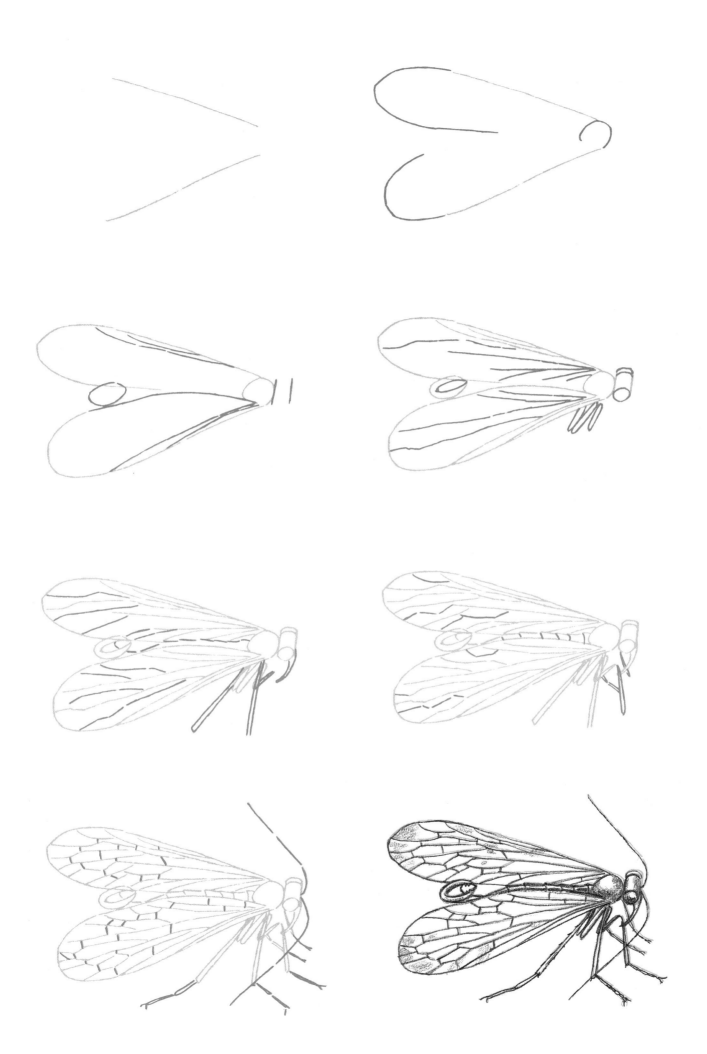

Scorpion Fly

Head Louse

Horntail

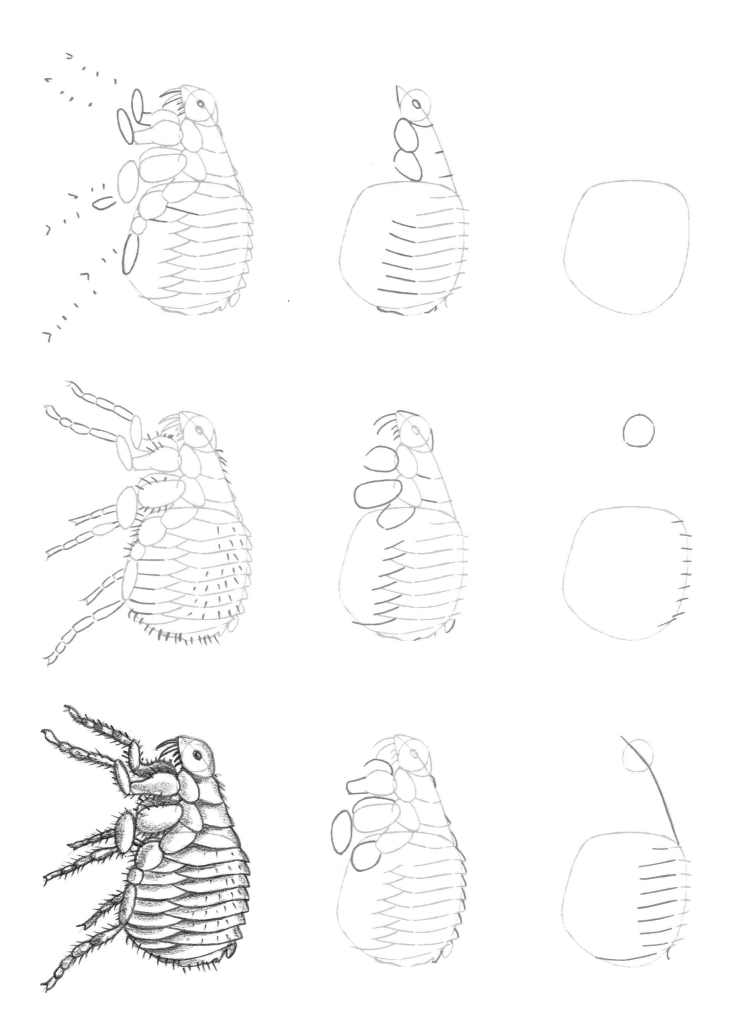

Dung Beetle

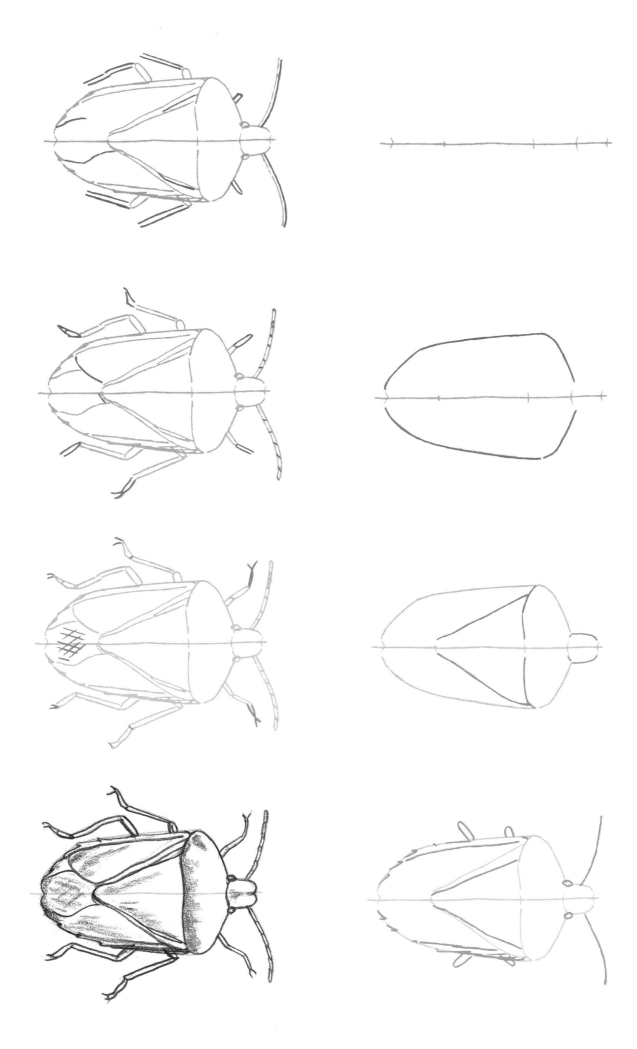

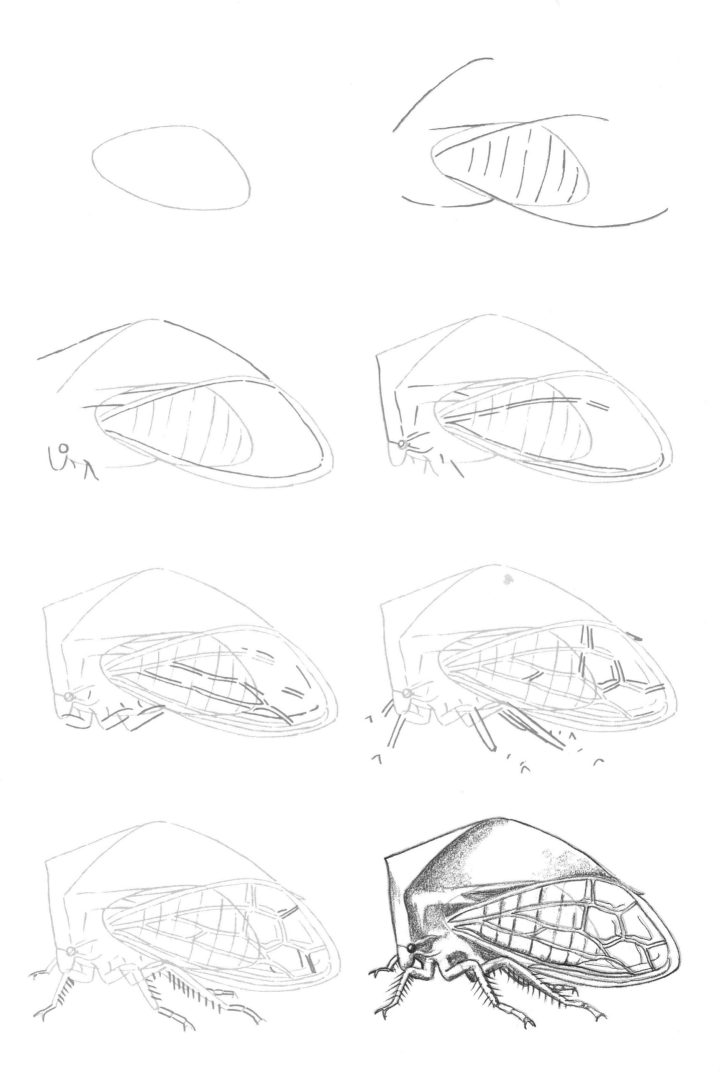

Buffalo Treehopper

Black Widow Spider

Tarantula

Wolf Spider

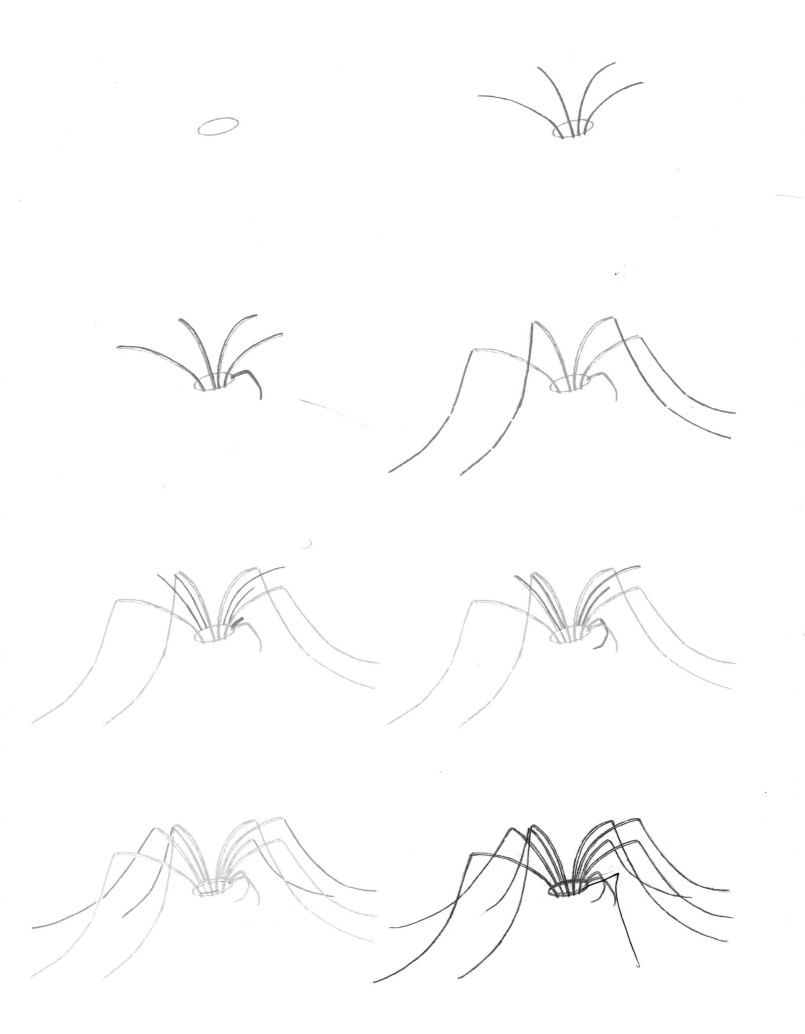

Daddy Longlegs

Slug

Snail

Scorpion

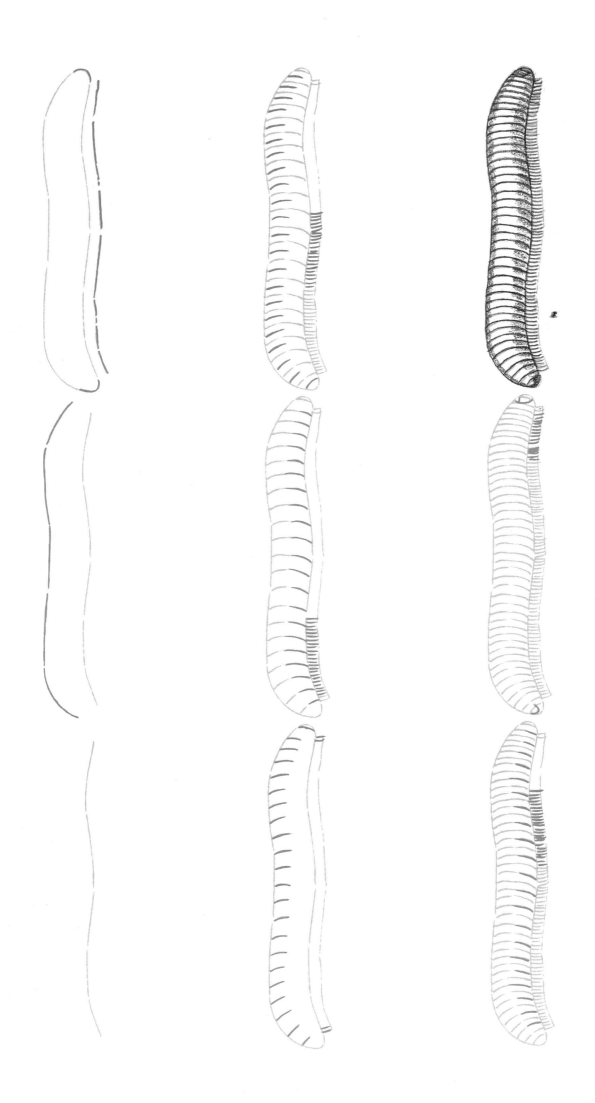

Millipede

Centipede

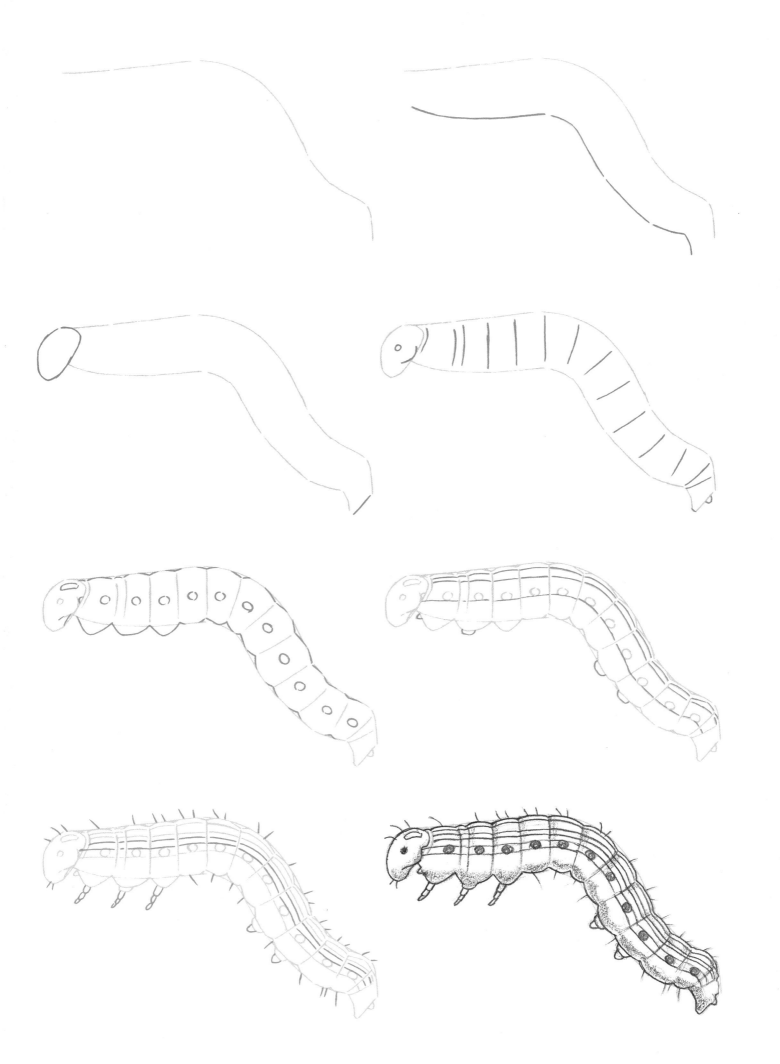

Caterpillar

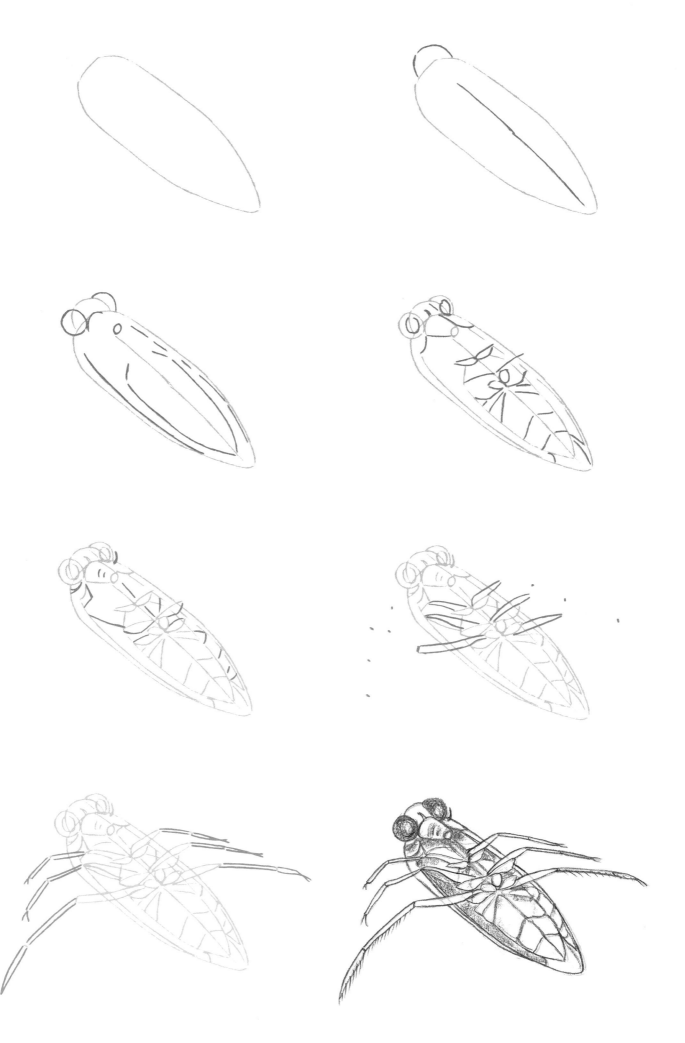

Back Swimmer

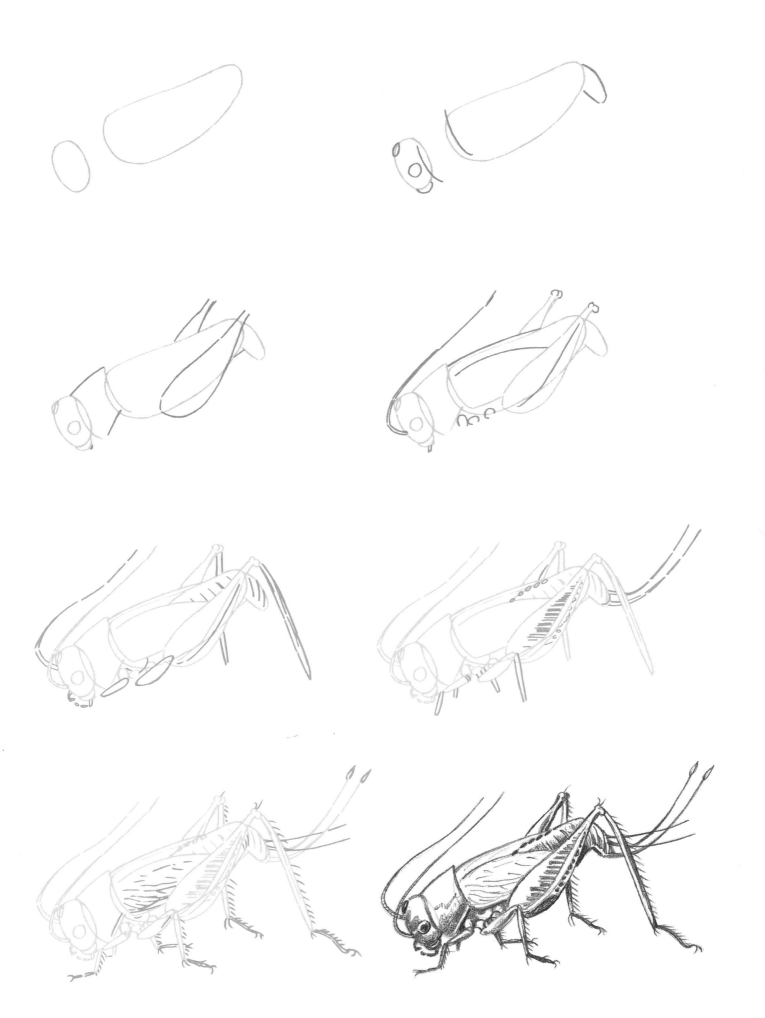

Field Cricket

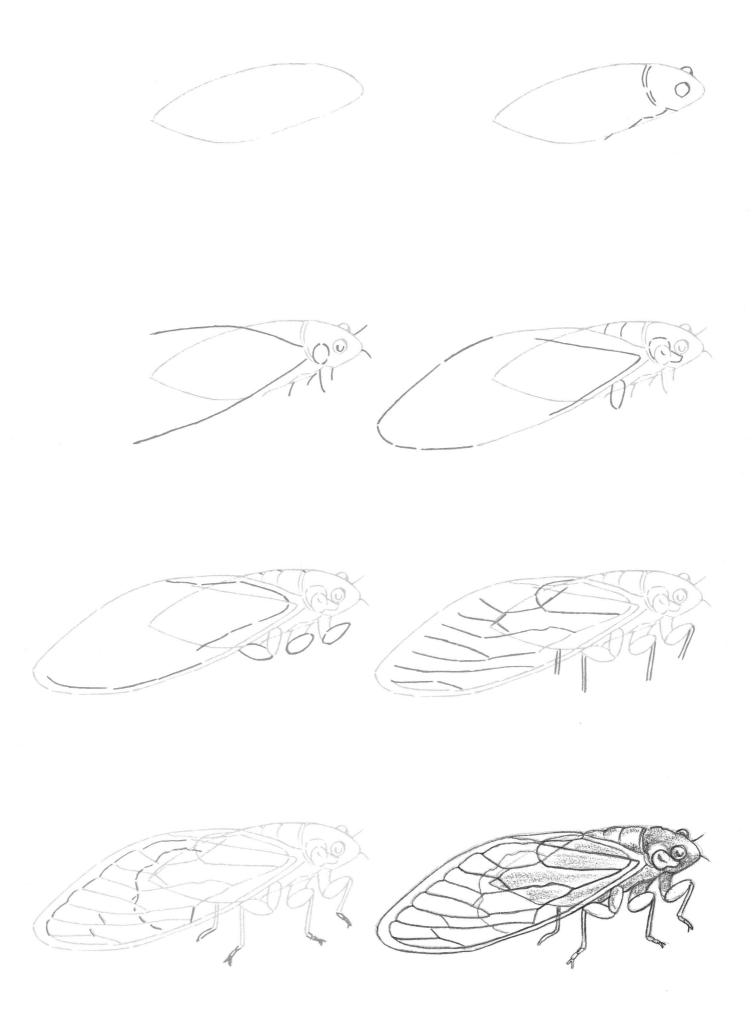

Cicada

Water Strider

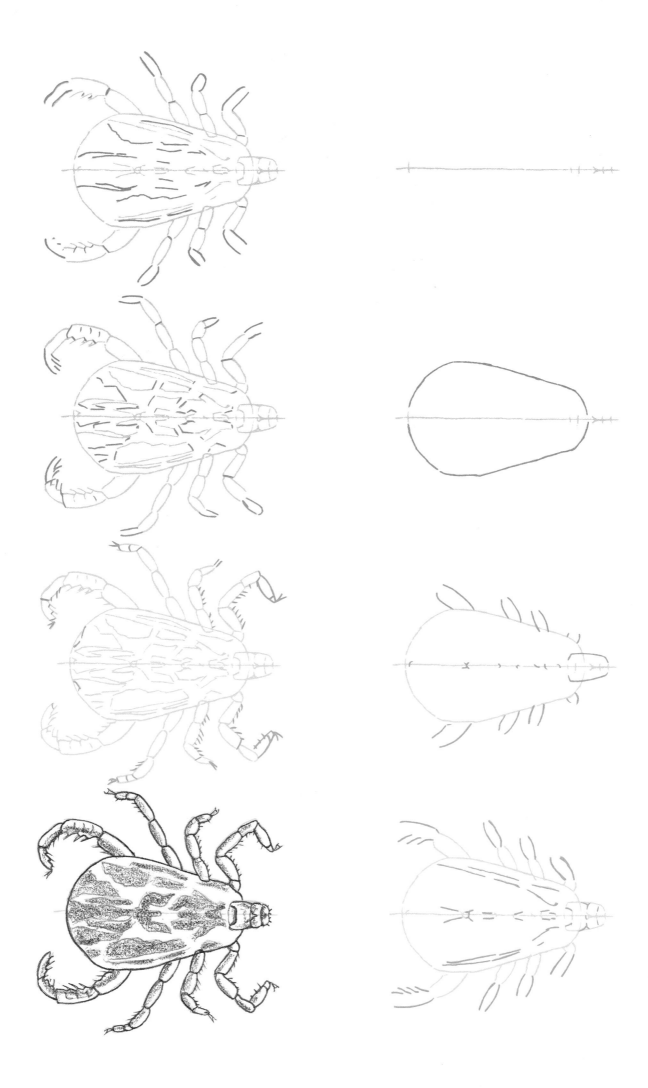

Lee J. Ames has been "drawing 50" since 1974, when the first "Draw 50" title—*Draw 50 Animals*—was published. Since that time, Ames has taught millions of people to draw everything from dinosaurs and sharks to boats, buildings, and cars. There are currently twenty titles in the "Draw 50" series, with nearly two million books sold.

Ames divides his time between Long Island, New York, where he runs an art studio, and Southern California. At the moment, he is working on a new drawing series for very young children.

Ray Burns has worked as a freelance illustrator since 1966. During that time he has illustrated close to seventy children's books, worked as a cartoonist, and created storyboards for television.

An ex-naval officer, Ray currently lives in Wilton, Connecticut, with his wife and their three children.

Date Due

MAY 0 3 2000		
MAY 2 4 2000	2 5 2006	
OCT 2 5		
DEC		6
JAN		
MAY		